Darth Maul

The epic begins . . .

STAR WARS ®
EPISODE I
THE PHANTOM MENACE™
By Patricia C. Wrede
Based on the screenplay and story by George Lucas

See Episode I through their eyes . . .

STAR WARS ®
EPISODE I
JOURNAL
Anakin Skywalker
Queen Amidala
Darth Maul
. . . and more to come

Before there was *The Phantom Menace*, there was . . .

STAR WARS ®
JEDI APPRENTICE
#1 The Rising Force
#2 The Dark Rival
#3 The Hidden Past
#4 The Mark of the Crown
#5 The Defenders of the Dead
#6 The Uncertain Path
. . . and more to come

STAR WARS

EPISODE I

JOURNAL

Darth Maul

JUDE WATSON

LUCAS BOOKS

SCHOLASTIC INC.

NEW YORK TORONTO LONDON AUCKLAND SYDNEY
MEXICO CITY NEW DELHI HONG KONG

ISBN 0-439-13941-4

Book designed by Madalina Stefan.

12 11 10 9 8 7 6 5 4 3 2 1   0 1 2 3 4 5 6/0

Printed in the U.S.A.

First Scholastic printing, March 2000

Darth Maul

You may think I am evil. I am not. I am efficient.

I serve my Master and the glorious Sith tradition. We are no less powerful for being hidden. We grow in the darkness. We gain strength from it.

We circle our enemy, the Jedi, and they do not know it. We laugh at what they think of as their power. Fools and liars, the Jedi think they have tapped the strength of the Force. Yet they ignore the dark side. It is their most profound mistake, the deepest foolishness of their order.

They say: *We do not seek power.* Yet they have it. Why do so many in the galaxy admire the Jedi?

Because the Jedi tell them to.

But one day the galaxy will see where true strength lies.

This is why I have begun this journal. Someday I hope it will be included in the Sith Archives, joining the stories and legends of the most glorious Sith Lords.

I have served my Master faithfully. I have been on many missions. But this mission is different. My Master's plan goes beyond the puny planet of Naboo to take in the entire galaxy. The Jedi will be called in at some point. The galaxy is full of cowards who look to the Jedi to help them cope. We are prepared for this.

I look forward to it.

On this mission, the Sith will reveal themselves to the Jedi at last.

We will devour them.

My Master has called me to Coruscant, to a secret place where I remain hidden, waiting for him to summon me.

I do not mind waiting. I use my time wisely. Waiting time is training time. Every minute of my life is devoted to learning the glorious Sith tradition as well as hard physical training. I keep myself in a constant state of readiness. When I meet the Jedi I will be at the peak of my power. I will be the strongest fighter in the galaxy.

Every training exercise has value, even the most basic ones. For example: One of the earliest training exercises taught by my Master consisted of running up a wall. I started from one end of the training room and ran toward the wall. I took several steps up the wall with my momentum and then flipped over to land on my feet. I did it over and over, even as my leg muscles burned with fatigue. If I missed, I could have broken my neck. Still, I continued. There is no fear in a Sith. Training drives out fear. The greatest thing I have learned about the Sith tradition is to be prepared to lose my life at any time.

When I was a boy, this was a basic exercise I could not master. I suffered many blows on the head and shoulders as, without the necessary strength, I fell backward. I would try to cushion my fall with my hands.

Never break a fall, my Master would say. *If you are prepared to break your fall, you are prepared for the fall itself. Sith do not fall. They do not fail.*

So, unable to break the fall, the next time I would fall more painfully than before. Soon my body was covered with bruises.

My Master would say this: *There is no pain where strength lies. Do it again.*

My head spinning, my bones aching, my legs trembling, I would do it again. And again I would fall.

There is no pain where strength lies. Say it!
There is no pain where strength lies, Master.
Do it again!

Each part of my training prepared me, and now I reap the benefits of my struggle. Now I never fall.

I run, I take four, five, six steps up the wall, and I flip through the air to land on my feet.

When I complete my basic exercises, I power up my double-bladed lightsaber and practice maneuvers. My body is as strong as durasteel and as fluid as water. I shift from one position of attack to another. I fall on one knee and slash my lightsaber as I imagine cleaving my victim cleanly. I roll away and grip my lightsaber with both hands for a vertical sweep. I leap and twist and come down, leading with my left shoulder. I deliver a death blow and leap away, somersaulting in the air. I perform ten thousand slashes, lunges, attacks.

My lightsaber is no longer a separate weapon, but part of my arm. I move in the time it would take my opponent to blink. I move in the time he would take to raise his weapon. He would only see the space where I had been. He would feel the sudden shock of the blow that would knock him to the floor.

I do these maneuvers a hundred times a day. I do them even though my body knows them intimately, even though I have not made a mistake or a misstep in years. I do them until the memory of the movement is part of the muscle itself. The goal of the Sith is to fight without thought.

There is no pain where strength lies.

I end with a triple backward flip. My breathing is

ragged, my muscles on fire. You may think I would quit. I never quit. I am just beginning.

But I am signaled on my comlink. My Master calls me.

I wear my comlink at all times, even when I'm sleeping. I am ready to serve in an instant.

I take the turbolift to my Master's secret strategy and communications room. He waits in the center of the room, in front of the holocomm monitors.

"The Neimoidians are signaling me," Lord Sidious tells me. He makes an irritated gesture. We do not have much confidence in the intelligence of the Neimoidians. They are useful, however. Their most important characteristic is their greed. We can exploit that for our own ends.

My Master has taught me that power used indirectly can be just as effective as a full-scale assault. We do not need to be on the front lines. We can hire fools to do our fighting. My Master controls their actions. He rules through fear and intimidation. It never fails. One day we will rule openly. But until then, we will use others to conquer.

My Master has not shared every detail of his plan with me, but he has shared more than usual. I know that his alliance with the Trade Federation is merely the first step toward his larger goal.

The peaceful planet of Naboo is now suffering under a blockade. The Neimoidians who run the Trade Federation seem to be the culprits. But it is my Master who pulls the strings.

The blockade will be followed by an invasion. The Neimoidian ships are crammed with battle droids and equipment. They only wait for a signal from Lord Sidious.

First, the vulnerable Queen Amidala must sign a treaty with the Trade Federation. It is better if the actions of the Trade Federation have at least the illusion of legality. Then Lord Sidious will begin to consolidate his power throughout the galaxy. His vision goes beyond one insignificant planet.

I am by his side. There are only two of us. That is enough, because we are Sith Lords. Our power is immeasurable, our range limitless.

"I want you to hear the transmission," my Master continues, raising his hood to cover his face. "No doubt they have contacted me because of some ridiculous setback that has sent them into a panic. Stay out of sight."

I move to the side.

The image of the Neimoidian coward Dofine fills the screen. Lord Sidious asks him impatiently what he wants.

Dofine blubbers, "This scheme of yours has failed, Lord Sidious. This blockade is finished! We dare not go against these Jedi."

I see my Master stiffen in anger. He doesn't like to be surprised, and the Jedi have entered the picture sooner than we thought they would.

But I feel a different emotion: pleasure. This means that my Master will have to call on me to fight them. Neimoidians are no match for Jedi.

I tell myself to control my anxious desire. If my Master senses it, he will rebuke me. I have been punished for my impatience in the past. I don't blame Lord Sidious for the punishments — they only made me stronger. Yet I do not want to invite them.

Dofine's whimpering doesn't help my Master's rage. The fool cries out that the blockade is finished. His panic makes him stupid.

I sense my Master's anger surge. I can only glimpse part of his face beneath the hood, but I recognize the signs. His mouth tightens. His anger is now like a living presence in the room. Not only have the Jedi been called in, but the Neimoidians are caving in at the first sign of pressure.

My Master's contempt paralyzes Dofine. He turns to the next Neimoidian in charge, Nute Gunray.

"I don't want this stunted slime in my sight again," he orders. We watch Dofine scurry off like a frightened child.

Even in small conflicts, I see I have much to learn from my Master. He uses his anger like an electro-jabber, to frighten and motivate. I must learn to use my anger as elegantly as I use my lightsaber. Finesse can never be overvalued.

He tells the Neimoidians to begin the invasion and does not listen to their protests. He then orders them to kill the Jedi immediately.

The screen goes black. Lord Sidious says nothing. I wait before speaking. If I interrupt my Master's thoughts, I will regret it. But the question burns on my lips, and at last I must ask it.

"Do you think the Neimoidians are capable of getting rid of the Jedi, Master? They are fools."

He nods slowly. "Yes, they are fools," he agrees. "But even fools can get lucky."

My relationship with my Master is complex. He rules me. He orders me and directs me. Yet we are both Sith Lords, and though I am his apprentice I share some of his power. As I have grown, so has his confidence in me. I stand by his side, but slightly behind, in his shadow.

I am content there. I still have much to learn. Not in battle, but in larger strategies. He sees weakness and exploits it. He senses anger and inflames it. His vision takes in a galaxy, with its multitude of planets and governments. The complexity doesn't intimidate him. He can hold it in his mind and know that someday, he will control it all.

When I return to my training room, I activate a panel to look out over Coruscant. The city spreads out above, below, and around me. It extends as far as I can see, curving to the horizon.

This is a favorite time of day for me, the last gasp of the strangled setting sun. Crimson flashes like splashes of blood off the millions of windows and metallic ships. The lights of the buildings illuminate the sky like a dozen moons. Even at night, Coruscant is never dark. The planet has no forests or mountains, and even its streams have been paved over and built on. It is a world made up of one city.

Billions of beings live on Coruscant in billions of dwellings. Yet here it is possible to have more privacy than on a sparsely populated planet. Among billions of beings, there are just as many ways to be secret. My Master Lord Sidious has created our lair, a world within a world. Around us throbs the city, but here we are invisible.

Out among those lights is the Jedi Temple. There the Jedi sit meditating while *we* act. They dream of a galaxy of justice and peace. It makes me smile to think of what they are about to face.

I cannot calm my eager, racing mind. I know the Neimoidians will fail to kill the Jedi. I will be called into service. All my life I've waited for this.

But wishing for the failure of the Neimoidians means that I am wishing that an order from my Master will fail. I don't like this contradiction. It borders on disloyal. But I can't help feeling it. The Jedi are *mine.* Mine to taunt, mine to destroy. I want my Master to see that I am a worthy apprentice. I've thought I'd been tested before. But this is my first true test. The ultimate test.

I strain my eyes, but the Jedi Temple is not visible from this viewpoint. I imagine it instead. I see a smoking ruin, a blasted shell. The bodies of fallen Knights and Jedi Masters are littered around it. I stand on the rubble before my Master.

Here is what I have done for you, Master.

I am pleased, Lord Maul.

I activate the panel, and it slides closed. The blinking lights of the city narrow to a slit, then disappear.

I must focus my mind. The Jedi are out there. I will meet them someday, and soon. I cannot bring the moment closer by wishing for it.

I feel some fatigue and hunger. That means I should undertake my most difficult training of the day. I push my body whenever I can. This I have learned from my Master. Events do not wait until you are well rested. You must be able to fight at the peak of your control even when you lack sleep and food.

It is time to activate the assassin droids.

Assassin droids are a necessary part of training. They are programmed to fight to the death. Blasters are built into their chests and hands. Their accuracy is perfect. A miscalculation on my part could be lethal.

I activate three droids and power up my double-bladed lightsaber. I am outnumbered, but assassin droids can't move as quickly as I can. They cannot jump, and their flexibility isn't as finely tuned.

Their weaponry makes up for that.

They track me easily in the empty room, their sensor lights flashing. I meet the first barrage and deflect it with my lightsaber, spinning it in a blur of motion while I track the next blaster fire and meet it. I can feel the power of the dark side. Aggression fuels it. The darkness throbs furiously, beating in my muscles, making me merciless and effective.

This is what I love: the feel of the dark side of the Force pulsing, growing, until the air crackles with the charge. It is the charge of blood and pain and anger. *I* control it. *I* manipulate it. It only makes me stronger.

The assassin droids are programmed to use complicated fighting strategies. They try a flanking maneuver, but I leap over them, the dark side fueling every muscle, and come at them from behind. I destroy the first droid as the second and third turn and fire.

I am already a millimeter away, escaping the fire and twisting to deliver a cleaving blow to the second droid. It topples, its sensor lights still flashing. I bury the other end of my lightsaber in its control panel. It lets out a screech of protest that sounds almost human. Smoke rises and I breathe it in. It is the smell of the Jedi Temple burning. The pleasure of destruction builds, makes my blood pound.

The third droid swivels. Instead of coming at me directly, it wheels to the right. I feel a start of surprise. It is a new maneuver. The droids are continually reprogrammed.

The maneuver and the surprise please me. I do a backward somersault as blaster fire pings over my head.

Challenge. That is a cornerstore of Sith training. Lord Sidious keeps me off balance.

This mission will challenge me. He told me that. I must not assume the Jedi will be easy to defeat. I must remember the power the dark side will give me. I must be confident, and I must be prepared.

Many times in the past, Lord Sidious gave me duties to perform without telling me the reason why. But now my Master includes me in communications with the Neimoidians. This must mean that he's come to trust me completely. He has come to see how valuable I am.

The blaster fire is close, closer than I like. I can feel the heat on the sleeve of my tunic. I smell singed material. The assassin droid has suddenly flipped sideways and aimed from the chest. I've been distracted.

Anger rises in me, which is good. The darkness crests and roars. I twist in the air, my lightsaber twirling, revolving. Its balance is perfect in my hand. I strike one hard blow to the left flank of the droid. I feel the power of the move reverberate all the way to my shoulder. It gratifies me. The other blow to the right follows a fraction of an instant later, so close that an observer would not be able to tell which blow came first. They would only see the armless droid wobble, its internal balance mechanism destroyed.

It is an easy job to slice off its head. The droid crashes to the floor, now a useless heap of smoking metal. I kick it out of my way with a smile, my lightsaber held loosely in my fingers. One day I will see a Jedi at my feet just like that.

Suddenly, my lightsaber is gone. It flies from my hand across the room. It lands in the hand of my Master.

I never see him enter. Not if he doesn't want me to.

The smile of triumph fades from my face.

"Do you think," Lord Sidious says, walking toward me, "you can ever relax your guard?"

"No, Master." What a clumsy, weak mistake. I should be prepared for him to enter at all times. How could I have forgotten that, even for a moment?

The lightsaber whirls in the air, twirling, held in

my Master's hand. I can't track it, it moves so fast. But I know it's heading for me.

Lord Sidious moves faster than my eye can follow. I smell heat and smoke. The laser traces the outline of my body, my face, my hands. The buzz is loud in my ear. One flinch, one involuntary twitch of a muscle, and I am dead.

I do not flinch.

At last, Lord Sidious deactivates my weapon. He tosses it toward me. The sweat on my palm almost causes me to drop it.

"Do not let me see you relax your guard again," my Master says. His eyes burn. "You are valuable, yes. But you are not indispensable, Lord Maul. I can do without you."

A flick of his robe, and he is gone.

I feel my leg muscles shudder as I lower myself to my haunches. I breathe slowly, in and out, until I am calm again. He is right. I will not let it happen again.

It is the Jedi's fault that I failed my Master. I pictured a Jedi at my feet, and I allowed myself to be distracted. Now I focus my mind on the Jedi, funneling my hatred and anger into a blade directed at them. The hatred is a hard, cold place, yet it burns. They are my enemy, and I will beat them because I am better, stronger, and smarter. I have weapons they don't have. I have my anger. And my most important weapon: I have no mercy.

I remember one of the first lessons my Master gave me on the Jedi:

Do not underestimate the Jedi. Even though they have a fatal flaw, they are formidable.

What is their fatal flaw, Master?

Compassion.

1 did not always live here. I'm told by my Master that I come from Iridonia. That world means nothing to me. I have no curiosity about my home planet. I could travel there to see where I came from, but what would be the point? I am interested in what I am, and what I will become. My life before I was a Sith is meaningless.

What was my name? I don't know. It doesn't matter. My former name represents a death, not a life. I died and was born into the Sith. I was found by my Master and taken as a baby. My parents might have looked for me. But no one in the galaxy can track a Sith who doesn't want to be found. They were powerless.

Another lesson from my Master:

The feelings of the powerless do not matter.

The feelings of those with power can be exploited.

My Master saved me. Without him, I would have been a superior being trapped in an ordinary life. He recognized even then the latent power within, the fury that raised me above all others, even as a young child. He showed me how the dark side makes that power flourish and grow. Tapping into anger and aggression fuels us. Someday I will grind that fact into the startled faces of the Jedi.

Our tradition is rich and deep. The Sith are an order almost as old as the Jedi. Our founder was a Jedi Knight who saw the truth — he knew that ignoring the dark side of the Force was foolish. Embracing it was the key to power. The Council did not have his vision. Cruelly, they banished him.

He did not slink away like a thief. He began the Sith order and enticed others to join. He planned to build an order that would defy the Temple itself. It did not take long for others to see his wisdom and leave the Temple to join him.

It was a glorious beginning. The only mistake the Sith made in the early years was that they allowed their members to become *too* powerful, *too* cunning. When you base an order on the idea of supreme domination, you create problems. The Sith Lords plotted against one another. Eventually, they destroyed one another.

But the last Sith was the smartest of all. It was he who devised the brilliant strategy that has kept us secret for a thousand years and allowed us to grow in the shadow of the dark side.

The genius of the strategy was its simplicity. *Only two.* Only two Sith are allowed to exist at one time — Master and apprentice.

It is because of our strength that we can do this. We don't need a Temple full of brats to nurse and train. We don't need a Council full of whining debaters. We don't need a corps of Knights to poke their noses into business that doesn't concern them just to inflate their own egos. Two of us are enough.

My earliest memories are of my Master. I learned discipline as soon as I learned to walk. If my Master deprived me of food or shelter in order to teach me, it was always a lesson of great value. If I was confined, if I was ignored, if I suffered, it doesn't matter. A child cries when his belly is empty, when he hears a food cart rattle by his door, smells his dinner, and yet the food cart rolls on. He does not understand that this pain makes him stronger.

A punishment is a lesson, young Maul. Learn it well.

I soon learned not to cry.

Here is an example of the good my punishments did me. I was a small boy, no higher than my Master's hip. Often I was taken to a desolate planet for outdoor exercises. There I learned how to use the dark side of the Force. Once during my training in a desolate field, a dinko surprised me. It is a nasty, palm-sized creature with sharp fangs and an aggressive disposition. Its twin grasping claws have been known to grab onto a finger or nose of a victim and not let go.

The dinko secretes stinking venom when startled. When I came across it, I flinched, and the venom sprayed against my face, stinging my eyes. I howled, then stomped it with my boot. I looked over at my Master, pleased at my courage.

"You flinched," he said. "You were afraid of the dinko?"

"Yes, Master," I answered. "But I controlled my fear." I said this with the certainty of the child that I was. My Master nodded, but I knew he was displeased.

I knew a punishment would come. Yet that evening I ate my usual meal. I was not confined in the sensory deprivation suit. I was not forced to sleep on the hard floor. The heat was not turned off.

It was the same the next day, and the next. Nothing disturbed my routine. Finally I forgot about the incident. I was young.

Then one night after a particularly exhausting day I went to my quarters. My door hissed closed. I undressed in the darkness and turned back the coverlet on my mat. A dinko jumped straight at me.

Startled, I batted it away, but I missed it when I tried to stomp on it. I hesitated, afraid its claws would tear into my bare foot. Then another dinko jumped out from a corner. Then another. And another. The room was filled with them.

Frantic, I ran to the door. It would not open. The lights would not work. In the darkness one dinko jumped on my shoulder and dug its claws into my ear. Another latched on to a toe. I cried and screamed, trying to shake them off. The venom blinded me. I bounced against the walls, trying to crush them. The stench of their venom turned my stomach.

It took me a long time to kill them all. In the morning my door opened and my Master stood there. He saw my inflamed skin, my swollen eyes, my bloody hands and feet. The stench of my room rolled out at him.

"Do not flinch again," he said.

The punishment is a lesson. My Lord Sidious taught me well. There could be no better teacher. Look at the result — my body is hard, and my mind is harder.

Always remember, my apprentice: Anger is a living thing. Feed it and it will grow.

I learned to see through the eyes of my Master. He showed me the galaxy and explained it in terms of power — who had it, who did not. He showed me that vast resources are there for the taking. The concerns of most beings are petty. Food and shelter are nothing. Love or devotion to a fellow being, a world, or a cause is not only a distraction but a danger, for it can be used against you. I have seen my Master use that weakness in others for his own ends. Did you know that there are those willing to die for someone they love? So puzzling.

I am willing to die for my Master, of course. But he is not just a being. He is a tradition, a heritage, an ideal. Someday I will be Master and have my own apprentice. He will be willing to die for me.

I am ready for whatever honor my fate chooses to show me. If my Master does not survive this mission, I will take over the role of Master and find my own apprentice. I am prepared.

Of course he will survive. But if he does not, I will not shrink from the task of achieving the same greatness. I have trained all my life for it.

The next contact from the Neimoidians doesn't take long in coming. When my Master summons me, he has a look of irritation on his face. He dons his hooded robe. No one but me can know his identity.

Remember, Maul: What is done in secret has great power.

"Remain in the background," Lord Sidious directs me. "I may need you. Who knows what those Neimoidian slugs have managed to bungle this time."

He summons the ship. I stay out of the range of the hologram device. My heart beats faster. Have the Neimoidians succeeded in killing the Jedi ambassadors?

Nute starts out with the good news.

Those who serve you always start out with good news. Do not be blinded by their self-congratulation. The more they blather, the more they are trying to cover their mistakes.

Nute tells my Master about the Trade Federation's successes. They control the cities in the north and west of Naboo. Thousands have been rounded up. They are searching for settlements that might contain pockets of resistance, but these pockets are isolated and small. Nute puffs up with his success, but his eyes dart nervously. When you rule by fear, you come to recognize the signs.

Lord Sidious directs him to destroy all the high-ranking officials quietly. Then he asks if Queen Amidala has signed the treaty.

There is a fraction of hesitation before Nute responds. I recognize the sign of an underling reluctant to impart bad news. My Master waits, saying nothing.

Queen Amidala has disappeared. Her ship got past the blockade.

This is worse news than we expected. How could the Neimoidians have bungled such an easy job?

"I want that treaty signed!" my Master thunders.

Impossible, Nute protests, his eyes glassy with fear. The ship is well out of their range. . . .

My Master controls himself. It is time to address the situation, find a solution.

"Not for a Sith," my Master responds.

Yes, not for a Sith. He motions to me, and I step forward. Lord Sidious tells the Neimoidians my name, and that I will find the lost ship.

I see the look of surprise and dismay on Nute and his officer Rune Haako's ugly faces. They try to conceal it, but nothing can be concealed from a Sith.

Lesser beings can consolidate your power for you, and sometimes, they can amuse you. Nute and Rune look at my warrior markings and my horns, and try not to back away from the image. I give them my fiercest look. A savage appearance can strike fear in the hearts of the weak. You don't have to say a word.

Nute looks from Darth Sidious to me.

Yes, fools. There are two of us.

My Master cuts the transmission. "Those incompetents have performed worse than my lowest expectations," he tells me. "Queen Amidala *must* sign that treaty." His face is taut with his rage. "The Jedi are behind this, of course. They are becoming a nuisance and must be eliminated. Find them."

I've been waiting for just this moment. "I will find them, Master," I tell him. "I will not fail."

Finding the Jedi and Queen Amidala in a vast galaxy doesn't worry me.

The Sith have many methods of tracking, some of which I cannot reveal, even in my own journal. Connection traces, instinct, logic, bribes, our own brilliance . . . our resources are many. Our range is as vast as the galaxy. My Master has shown me time and again that there is nothing too small to escape his notice, no system far enough out of reach, no ship that can't be found if you have the patience and cunning to look.

It doesn't take us long to narrow the search to one small planet in the Outer Rim Territories: Tatooine. It won't take long to find the precise co-ordinates of the landing site. They are in our grasp.

Lord Sidious summons me, and I come to his side. Together we look out over the lights of Coruscant. I know my Master feels the same exhilaration I do.

He has planned carefully, step by step. Caution. Guile. Subterfuge. Hidden motives, secret acts. I have watched my Master use all of these to get to this point. Now at last we will have no need to hide our power.

"They have accepted a communication from Sio Bibble," Lord Sidious tells me. "They haven't answered it. But we can be reasonably sure that they're still on Tatooine."

"Tatooine is sparsely populated. If the trace was correct, I will find them quickly, Master."

Lord Sidious tells me that I have been well trained, and the Jedi are no match for me. Although I know this already, it gratifies me to hear it. My Master does not praise me often.

"At last we will reveal ourselves to the Jedi," I say. "At last we will have revenge."

"It is too late for them to stop us now," my Master agrees, his voice soft. I can feel the strength ripple underneath the purr, the cruelty, the hard purpose that fires my own. "Everything is going as planned," he continues, his eyes on the vast city. "The Republic will soon be under my control."

And mine, Master. For I stand by your side.

I leave my Master and hurry to the concealed landing platform. My transport is always ready.

My Sith Infiltrator is not a large craft, but it has a powerful hyperdrive. Time is crucial now. We feel quite certain that the Queen's ship sustained some damage while escaping the blockade. There can be no other reason for landing on such a desolate planet in the Outer Rim. I suggested that Queen Amidala might be hiding out while she makes plans to retake her planet, but Lord Sidious shook his head.

"She is not so brave," he said. "She still trusts the power of the Senate. No, that is not why they landed on Tatooine. And the reason is not your concern. Just find them."

When I come out of hyperspace, I pick up a distress signal from a nearby ship. I ignore it. I always ignore distress signals. What are the petty problems of others next to my mission?

Soon I can see the ship on my viewscreen. It is a small space cruiser stalled in a shipping lane. The distress signal grows more frantic as I pass it by. Someone pleads for help. Let the Jedi come to the aid of pathetic ships. Sith have more important tasks.

Suddenly, a large bulk freighter appears out of hyperspace. At first I assume it is coming to the aid of the stalled ship. But to my surprise, the stalled ship suddenly wheels around and heads straight for me, the bulk freighter maneuvering into position on the other side. They surround me in a pincer movement. Panels slide back, and I see that the innocent-looking bulk freighter is equipped with proton torpedoes.

Then I understand. Pirates. Togorian pirates, most likely. The fiercest and the most ruthless in the galaxy.

I beat the console with my fist. Fool! I should have been on my guard. How could I have left myself open like this? They have me surrounded.

Now that they have seen me, I must kill them. The mission is too important to have witnesses.

I try a series of maneuvers to slip between or around them. The bulk freighter quickly veers to cut me off. The cruiser dogs my flank. Togorians are expert pilots. A chase or late activation of the cloak would only draw more attention.

Nothing is a sufficient reason for failure.

All of these calculations run through my mind in swift seconds as the first ship fires at me. I have set the deflection shields, but the blow rocks the ship alarmingly. They have powerful weapons. I'm sure the shot was meant as a warning.

There is only one recourse.

I cut power. The ship hangs, stalled. I turn off the deflection shields.

It's a slight gamble, but I'm rarely wrong. The next shot from the proton torpedoes could turn me and the ship into space dust. I wait, withdrawn back on the bridge so they can't see me, even with electrotelescopes. The fools are most likely puzzled and wary.

The smaller decoy ship heads toward me. No doubt they mean to board my ship and kill all aboard. They haven't fired again because they want the ship, too. The Sith Infiltrator is impressive. They haven't seen anything like it before.

Irritation courses through me at this interruption. I will defeat them, but it will take time.

I race to the back of the ship. I activate the release for the escape pod and climb inside. The pod is smaller than most. It has barely enough room for me.

I wait until I see the pirate ship approach. Then I slide the release and drift out into space. I keep the engine on low power and hug the hull.

When I'm sure the pirates have all boarded, I take off, carefully keeping my ship between me and the bulk freighter. The freighter has drawn closer, greedily awaiting the outcome. They think that those aboard are prepared to surrender.

I could escape them easily and pilot the pod to Tatooine. But I will not surrender my ship.

I head for the pirate ship, straight into the heart of my enemy. A shipload of space pirates is no match for me. I will ram their greed down their throats.

They will live to regret an attack on a Sith.

I ease my craft around the hull of the bulk freighter. These ships are not built for graceful speed. They are basically boxes with hyperdrives. This ship is uglier than most. It is caked with grime and space dust. The hull is battered and pock-marked with cannonfire.

The docking bay is open, no doubt in preparation to receive my captured ship. I fly into the opening and land. The docking bay looks worse than the ship's exterior. Against the walls are stacked metal containers that spill their contents onto the filthy floor. Spare parts are simply dumped in greasy piles. The remains of meals are scattered about, as though the pirates drop bones and food when they are finished. The lights are only on half-power, leaving the corners in deep shadow.

My Master told me once that the greedy are the

first to economize. He has never been proven wrong.

There are only two pirates in the docking bay. Togorians are tall beings of great strength, covered in fur that the pirates wear long and matted. Their claws are fierce and sharp. The pirates use their claws to slit open crates to see what is inside. When they hear my ship, they look up, then look down again. They assume that a fellow pirate has landed the pod.

What stupidity. This will be too easy.

I register all this, but I do not see beings as others do. Under normal circumstances, I barely register other living creatures, unless they are threats or obstacles. When I go into battle they cease to be living beings at all. They become targets.

I open the hatch and leap out of the pod to charge them, my lightsaber activated. The targets freeze for an instant, but then they move fast. Roaring and spitting, they grab weapons from a pile near them. The dull-witted cretins don't use strategy; they just rush at me like barbarians, one with a vibroblade, the other with a vibro-ax. The one with the ax is clumsy. The other favors his left side.

I see all this as I leap. At the crest of my arc, my lightsaber is high in the air. I twist slightly to attack the first pirate from his right side. When the lightsaber comes down on his shoulder, it has all the force of my body behind the blow. He goes down with a surprised grunt, his arm and vibro-blade clattering to the floor. I deliver another blow, piercing his chest, and he is still.

I move aside as the second pirate wields his vibro-ax. I am fluid as water and slip through his opening like a breeze. He grunts in frustration at his inability to touch me. This pirate is bigger than the first, taller than I am. His fur gives off a rank, sour smell.

Then he surprises me. Instead of coming at me, he wheels around and runs. I realize quickly that he's heading for the comlink station near the door. I can't have that. I can't have him alert the entire ship to my presence.

Move in secret, when you can. The blow in the darkness is the killing blow.

I draw in the power of the dark side. I focus it toward the pirate. It sends him flying past the station. He hits the wall with a dull thud.

He turns, staggering, and roars at me in rage. Then he charges. I am expecting this, of course. I wait for his momentum to make him clumsy as he begins his strike an instant too soon. It is easy for me to evade the blow. When he totters, I whip around, my lightsaber twirling, and neatly sever his hand from his wrist. His eyes widen in surprise as he gazes down at the empty place where his hand once was. Then he feels the pain.

The howl is earsplitting. I have to take care of him fast. One side of my lightsaber slices his neck. The other hits him as he crashes to his knees, then falls over, dead.

The targets have been eliminated, and I'm not even breathing hard.

I race toward the bridge down filthy corridors crammed with discarded goods. I meet no one. Pirate ships are not crowded. Togorians are known for their aggressive natures. If too many of them are aboard one ship, fights break out. They have no discipline. Only greed.

I pause just outside the opening to the bridge. I have moved so quietly that no one has heard my approach. When I'm in attack mode, I am nothing more than a shadow.

The bridge is even more cluttered than the docking bay. Through the dim light I see discarded cartons, their contents flung on the floor. Items the pirates did not think valuable enough to paw through: console boards, clothing, survival gear. Swinging from chains overhead in gruesome decoration are giant cages filled with creatures who gape at me, wild-eyed. I realize that they've been stuffed, their expressions frozen at the moment of their deaths. I see surprise, horror, pain, rage.

If only there were a few Jedi among them.

This time there are four targets. I can smell them as well as see them. The Togorians are intently watching the console, where a fierce-looking pirate is reporting back from my ship. His fur is elaborately braided and ornamented with glittering objects.

One of the Togorians appears to be the captain. He wears a necklace of skulls from various beings. I wait, listening.

"I'm telling you, there's no one on board!" the pirate onscreen roars angrily. "Of course we searched for hidden compartments, we're not fools! It's an unmanned ship. The course was set for Tatooine. That's why it didn't answer the distress signal. Have you ever seen a ship like this? I haven't!"

The Togorian in charge appears to be thinking. "All right, idiot," he growls finally. "Bring both ships into the loading dock. The bay is still open. If you do find any passengers, kill them."

He cuts the communication. One of the other pirates turns to him. "Hela-Tan is a fool," he mutters in the Togorian low growl. "They could be hiding."

"Then we'll find them," the other replies.

"Or they could have escaped," a third pirate speaks up.

"Shut your flapping mouth. What's the difference? We have the ship." The Togorian captain turns away, unconcerned.

That's my cue. Everything on the bridge fades to gray — the screens, consoles, cages, open containers, discarded food. They are only obstacles or objects to be used, background to my targets. Even while the pirates have been speaking, my mind has been strategizing. I will move without thought, kill without mercy. And I will do it faster than those lumbering Togorians can take a breath.

I am in the room and have dispatched the first target before the others are even aware of my presence. He goes down without a cry, the victim of a ceiling-to-floor sweep from my lightsaber that cuts him in two.

The thud of his massive body hitting the floor alerts the others. The captain turns and sees me. Roaring, he bares his fangs.

"Prepare to die, scum," he screams, reaching down and coming up with a vibro-ax in each hand.

Sorry, cretin. I'm not impressed. Why do my opponents announce their intentions with threats and taunts? Do they really think they can intimidate me? I never speak in a battle. It is a waste of energy. I prefer to concentrate on the joy of killing.

I ignore the captain for the moment. He is several steps away, and I can accomplish much in a few steps. I will leave him for last. Let him see what I do to his crew. I am already flipping in a midair roll to take the second pirate. The dark side propels me across the bridge, and I kick the target in his windpipe, sending him flying back. He makes a gurgling sound, unable to scream, and I see fear in his eyes. It sends a jolt of pleasure through me. He has never come across an opponent like me before. I deliver a fatal blow to the chest with the lightsaber, and he falls.

I see his life force ebb, and the dark side surges in me, pulsing, filling me. My aggression feeds on it ravenously, and I move even faster, even more efficiently, making not one mistake. I charge the third pirate with such ferocity he is unable to combat me. He waves his vibroblade, but it merely fans the air as he slashes ineffectually. I counter his moves before he can even manage to follow through on them. Then my lightsaber cuts him down.

The dark side alerts me that the captain is taking aim at my back. He will try to crush me with a swipe from each hand, hoping to cut me in two.

I leap, again using the dark side to add velocity and distance. I sail high above his head and grab onto one of the cages with one hand. I use the momentum to swing past the captain. I let go, make a midair reversal, and land behind him. I have done this so fast that his two vibro-axes are now meeting where my body once stood. They tangle, emitting a screeching sound that sends smoke spiraling upward. The cage above us swings crazily, sending grotesque shadows across the floor. The captain roars in frustration.

My jump has landed me behind him and slightly

to the left. It is my favorite angle of attack, though of course I am invincible from any position. He spins around to face me, already swinging his vibro-axes. They meet the handle of my lightsaber. Smoke rises, and I feel the pirate's strength shudder up my arm into my shoulder. I like a good adversary.

But I don't have time to play with this one. I flip backward and reverse direction, coming at the captain from the right. I slash his arm, rendering it useless. It dangles by his side, and the vibro-ax falls to the floor with a thud.

My blow has angered him. His eyes are filled with pain. I note this with glee and attack, my lightsaber a blur of red. He dodges one blow, catches the next, cries out. I move in for the kill. My blood pounds in my ears, mingles with the blood I have spilled. My lightsaber hums with my killing blow, a vertical sweep through the chest.

In seconds, he is on the floor, dead eyes glazed with surprise.

The comm unit crackles. "Approaching docking bay."

I whirl and hurry to the unit. I do not activate the visual monitor, but I speak clearly into the comm unit.

"Proceed to the bridge."

Then I get to work. My Sith training was extensive. My Master was concerned not only with my physical and intellectual perfection, but also my mechanical skills. Many times my knowledge of starship engines and various communication devices and weapons has come in handy.

This is such a time. It only takes me a few seconds to interface the propulsion units with the proton torpedoes.

In other words, as soon as the engine ignites, the ship will blow itself up. Togorians always leave the scene immediately to avoid capture. I don't think the deaths of their fellow pirates will slow them down. The returning pirates will most likely think the others killed each other in a brawl. Not an unusual occurrence among pirates.

I run for the docking bay, hoping to avoid contact with the pirates heading for the bridge. Not that I can't take them, but time is of the essence now. I must get aboard my ship and be well clear when the ship blows.

Of course, I could board my ship and take off for Tatooine without destroying the Togorian ship, but I don't like to leave those who attack me still standing, no matter how much in a hurry I may be. And my orders from my Master are strict: Do not attract attention. No one must know of the existence of the Sith.

I make it to the docking bay without being seen.

I have to duck into a side corridor as the pirates stumble by me, heading for the bridge, already quarreling about the division of the spoils.

I hurry across the cluttered bay. I immediately spot the sleek shape of the Infiltrator next to the bulky space cruiser. I'll have to leave my escape pod behind. It's unfortunate, but I can't take the time to load it.

The ramp is down, and I race up and spring inside. I nearly collide with a pirate who has stayed behind — the Togorian with the glittering objects braided into his fur.

I had underestimated the greed of the pirate. Of course he would fall behind to take the best of what he could for himself. His hands are full of the credits I keep for emergencies. I can see that a satchel at his feet is bulging, no doubt with the crystals I keep for worlds that do not accept credits.

He is just as surprised as I am. I see now that the objects twined in his fur are sharp razors. I realize that they could serve as effective weapons in a close fight. All the Togorian would have to do is fall on someone in order to slice them to ribbons.

I activate my lightsaber. With a grin, he drops the credits and takes his vibro-ax from his belt.

"There you are," he says, licking his lips with a thick purple tongue. "Think you can escape me? Think again. I'll finish the job."

There are those taunts again. I don't feel fear. But I do feel irritation. The rest of the pirates should be at the bridge now. Any moment they will start the engines. This detour is putting me in unnecessary danger.

We are at close quarters. I need to dispatch him quickly. He is big, bigger than the others, and stronger.

I whirl in an arc and go for his chest, but he is agile and sidesteps the attack. He misses my shoulder by a breath with his vibro-ax. It crashes down on the console. This won't do. I need a functioning ship. I leap past him and flip down the ramp, just out of reach of his vibro-ax. It clangs as it hits the ramp.

I turn for the attack, lunging at him as he jumps to the floor. This huge Togorian moves well. He shakes his fur, sending shards of light into my eyes. Momentarily dazzled, I lose my focus. I am in the middle of a vertical sweep when he twists, rolls, grunts, and comes up on my other side. I jump away, but the vibro-ax catches me on the leg.

The pain sends a red haze over my vision. He grins as he smashes one massive arm against my wounded leg. I feel the razors slice into my torn flesh. The pain sears me, but I bare my teeth at him in contempt.

If your enemy inflicts pain, do not allow him to see it. There is no pain where strength lies.

My rage is a torrent, a burning river. I leap, twist, keeping my weight on my good leg. My light-saber is part of my body now, merciless, hard, cruel. I dance around him, slicing his arms, chest, shoulders. I want a thousand cuts to kill him. He falls facedown without a cry.

I leap over his body and up the ramp. My leg wound screams in protest but I do not limp. I steel myself against the pain, disciplining my mind against it. I won't attend to it until I am safely away from this ship and have landed on Tatooine.

Then I hear the warm-up of the preliminary igni-tion of the freighter. I start my engines and acti-vate departure procedures. A warning light tells me that the hatch will not close. At that moment, I hear a roar. The pirate has wedged himself into the doorway. He is missing an arm. His face is smeared with blood and contorted with rage. I rec-ognize the look. He means to kill me before he dies.

Any moment, the freighter will blow.

I push the engines to full power and blast out of the landing bay. The Togorian is half in, half out, his bloody fingers clutching at the hatch door. His face snarls at me in gruesome determination.

I ram him with my head. His grip loosens. I kick his midsection. The pirate, incredibly, still hangs on. The dark side surges, fed with blood and rage. I tap into it, using it as I whirl and kick him solidly.

At the same moment, the freighter explodes in a shower of metal and debris.

The Togorian is blown from the hatch, but he is already dead. For a moment, his body is plastered against my viewscreen. I see a bloody cheek. An eye. One hand is still curled, gripping nothing. Then a split second later he spirals out into deep space. The shock-wave vibrations of the blast send the craft rocking.

I return to the pilot seat. It takes a moment before I can collect myself. My battles are seldom so closely won.

I plug in the coordinates for Tatooine. Night is falling on the planet, and lights wink on below. By the time the surface looms close enough for me to pick out features of the landscape, I am laughing, enjoying my favorite moment. I am safe, and my enemies are dead.

1 prefer night landings. Even if my Master hadn't decreed it, I would have chosen it. As I approach Tatooine, I can see the lights of the spaceports and the occasional solitary gleam of a moisture farmer's wretched dwelling. The lights tell me things the daylight cannot — the glare of the sun can hide, the sand can camouflage. But most creatures like to have lights at night. They reveal themselves.

The sky is an inky blue as I land on an isolated mesa near my first search quadrant, close to Mos Espa. First, I activate detectors to make sure no one is in the area. Lord Sidious has warned me specifically not to attract attention on this mission. The probe droids will conduct the search. I must stay with the ship.

The wind is cold as I hike to a nearby dune and climb to the top. I sweep the area with my electrobinoculars. I can just make out the spaceport of Mos Espa in the distance. There are other settlements nearby. I activate three probe droids and send them out. The probes have been downloaded with information on the Jedi. They will send back readings that will give me the coordinates of the Jedi's location.

By this time tomorrow, they will be dead at my feet.

I trudge back to the ship. The sand sucks at my boots, and, thanks to my injury, each step requires an effort. Fiery blasts radiate from the wound. Sweat beads up on my forehead.

I loathe weakness. It is time to tend to my wound now that the probes have been launched.

Before I begin to dress my wound, I meditate, focusing on the pain until it becomes fiercer. It becomes every dark thought, every savage feeling I have felt. It becomes a power I can use.

There is no pain where strength lies.

My Master has told me that the Jedi look at pain differently. They embrace it. They thank it for alerting them to the fact that they've been wounded and need to care for themselves. They think this helps them heal.

What fools they are. Pain is power. I will take my pain and I will use it against them.

When I meet the Jedi, I will be even stronger than before.

I delay applying bacta to the wound. I sit motionless, waiting out the pain until it becomes not pain, but desire. My need for revenge against the Jedi burns me. They have done this to me. My pursuit of them has brought me here. I pull the darkness around me like a hooded cloak. I surround myself with anger.

Only then do I dress the wound and apply bacta. I feel myself begin to heal.

As the night drags on, exhaustion from my battle with the pain that is not pain settles into my bones. I dress my wound again with bacta and bandages and stretch out on my sleep-couch. Despite my best efforts, my mind drifts. I remember back to the time I felt pain so searing I thought I would die from it. Pain so intense that I could not even remember my name.

That was the day I became a Sith.

It is years ago. I am old enough to feel that I am already full grown and mature, but young enough not to know what that means. I do not know how old I am, for my Master never told me how long ago it was when he took me, or what my age is. Age is of no consequence to a Sith. We live long lives. We do not track our development in such a mundane way.

So it is not my age that tells my Master I am ready, but my abilities. I know I am strong and fast and I never break. My control of the darkness that fuels the Force is close to perfect.

I am happy when my Master tells me I am ready to take the last tests that will allow me to become a Sith Lord. I have already fulfilled two years of missions for my Master. I have pleased him. I am ready.

For fourteen days, I take a series of physical tests. Lightsaber duels, endurance exercises, fasting. Some tests I take blindfolded or in a sensory-deprivation suit. It is the most grueling fourteen days I can imagine. By the time it ends, I am exhausted.

And I find that the test has not yet begun.

"I am sending you to a planet in the Outer Rim," my Master tells me. "It is made up of three kinds of terrain: desert, swamp, and mountains. You will have at least three matches on each terrain. I have sent a fleet of assassin droids to attack you. Each are programmed with different strategies. Some will work together, some will work alone. They are all programmed to kill."

That gets my attention.

"That is correct," Lord Sidious says quietly. "I am prepared to lose what I most value. So must you be to become a Sith. You must be prepared to lose your own life in order to win."

I nod. "I understand, my Master."

"You will have to survive for a month," Lord Sidious adds. "You will have only a survival pack."

Despite my exhaustion, I am exhilarated, too. Did I ever imagine it would be easy to become a Sith Lord? The value of anything is measured by effort. I will prove to my Master that I am the best apprentice in the history of the Sith. I shall not only survive, I shall conquer.

I realize now how young I was. I couldn't have known what was ahead of me.

I land on the planet and begin my test. It is infinitely more difficult than my imagination has been able to grasp. The assassin droids are relentless. Again and again I am awakened by an attack. Again and again I fight, move camp, fight again. I am driven into the mountain snows and across the burning desert. I lose my survival pack in a battle and have to kill and forage for food.

Ten days go by. Fifteen. Twenty.

I grow thin and my strength begins to ebb. I have never felt such weakness, even during my fasts. And yet I have to go on. I have to fight, I have to find a place to rest, I have to fight again. I count off the days in my head.

One battle with two assassin droids almost undoes me. I sustain a bad blaster wound to my thigh. I drag myself to a cave to hide. I have no bacta, no bandages. Yet I know I must recover before I fight again.

The wound festers. It is a searing, blinding pain. I am too weak to forage for food. The days blur. I no longer know how long I've been on the planet. Surely it has been more than a month. Has my Master forgotten about me?

I am close to hallucinating when Lord Sidious appears at the mouth of the cave. I am so glad to see him that my bones turn to water. I look at him hopefully.

"Now it is time for your final battle," he says.

Another battle? I can't even walk.

Yet his power over me is so strong that I rise on my watery legs. The cave walls shimmer in front of my eyes. My balance is off. I fumble for my lightsaber and activate it.

"Where is the assassin droid, Master?" I ask. My voice emerges hoarsely from thick, swollen lips. I need water. I would kill for water.

My Master powers up his lightsaber. "I will be your opponent."

I take a step toward him. I know this is my final test. I summon up the dark side of the Force. I take all my pain and anger and form it into a tightly packed ball. I set that ball aflame in my chest.

I feel a trickle of strength enter me. That encourages me. I use that strength to stoke the fire inside me.

"You cannot be as pathetic as you look," my Master says. He raises his lightsaber and attacks.

I parry the blow and reverse, come at him from the opposite side. But he is already gone by the time I am able to make my attack. The lunge throws off my balance. I weave, the cave walls blurring. He laughs.

"I take it back," he says. "You *are* that pathetic."

He tells me I am weak, not worthy of being a Sith Lord. He tells me he has misjudged me. I attempt to attack him. The ball of anger inside me turns to howling rage. It is painfully obvious that he is playing with me. He can kill me in a heartbeat. Yet something in me will not accept this, even from my Master. My life force won't allow it. I struggle on, even in the face of his laughter.

He tells me that he has expected my failure. He saw my weaknesses long ago. Secretly, over the long years, he has trained another apprentice. I have not been alone.

I point out, gasping, that more than one apprentice is against the rules of the Sith.

"You are right," he says. "A spark of intelligence at last."

The second apprentice is on the other side of the planet. He conquered all the assassin droids sent after him. He did not sustain more than a flesh wound. He is healthy and strong.

"Unlike the pathetic weakling I see before me," my Master says.

I realize dully what this means. My opponents had not really been the droids. My opponent had been someone I had never seen. My enemy has been chosen by my Master. *He* will become a Sith Lord. *He* will receive the honor I was due. *He* will reap the glory I had punished my body and disciplined my mind in order to receive.

A slow rage begins to burn through me. It is a terrible anger, no less fierce because it starts as a kernel of disbelief and then builds. I have never felt anything like it. I know it can consume me.

No. I can direct it. My rage will consume my enemy. It will consume my Master.

Yes, my Master is now my enemy. He is my betrayer. Hatred sears me, hardens me.

"Can you make the next leap in logic?" Lord Sidious asks me contemptuously. "Try to focus, Maul. If there can be only one apprentice, then one of you must die. Who do you think I have chosen to die, Maul?"

The rage rockets within me, pumping energy into my muscles. I can do anything. I can kill my Master. I *want* to kill him. My hatred is so huge it blots everything else but my desire for his blood.

With a howl torn from the depths of my belly, I spring at him. He barely misses the first blow from my lightsaber, for even in my rage I have employed strategy, coming at him from below, hoping to rip him in two.

He parries my next blow. Sweat stings my eyes as I move across the rough cave floor. I do not stumble. I am nothing but the pulse of my anger, pure energy, pure darkness. I streak across the cave floor and come at him again, somersaulting through the air. My lightsaber whirls in the darkness. When he parries the blow, he staggers.

I am going to kill him. Every beat of my blood exults in my power. Every blow I deliver is meant to be the killing blow. I use reserves of strength I did not know I had. My blows are sure and precise, my footwork flawless. I gather in the power of the dark side. I feel my power clash with his. The air is thick, charged with our dark, titanic powers.

He parries every blow. But I see that he has to work hard to keep me at bay. Triumph roars through me at my Master's weakness. He is not as powerful as he appears.

"You want to kill me?" he taunts. "You want to kill your Master?"

"Yes," I grunt.

"You hate me?"

"Yes!" I scream out the word through gritted teeth.

But I have been weakened by my ordeal, and my Master maneuvers me against the cave wall. I am gasping, trying to suck in enough air to keep going. My vision blurs as Lord Sidious raises his lightsaber. I parry the blow, but my lightsaber suddenly flies out of my hand, torn by the power of my Master directing the dark side. I realize then that he has just begun to tap into his own reserves. Mine are played out.

I will not be able to deflect the next blow. It will rend me in two. In a blur of heat and pain I see the mighty power of my Master raised against me, see the lightsaber come toward me, see my death as clearly as a bone-white moon in an ebony sky.

I lunge forward and sink my teeth into his hand. I strike like an animal, so quickly he doesn't have time to step away. I taste his blood and spit it back at him in contempt.

Yes, he will kill me. But I will die with his blood on my lips.

The lightsaber comes down. I wait for the pain and shock. I wait to die.

My Master laughs. He tosses the lightsaber aside. It is a training saber. It does not harm me.

I am alive. He will not kill me. My muscles fail me but I don't let him see it. I lean slightly against the cave wall in back of me. The rock bites into my back and I concentrate on the pain while my Master continues to laugh. I will never forget the sound of that laughter. There is no mercy in it.

"Do you feel the hate?" he asks.

I nod.

"It is the source of your strength. You still hate me," he says. "No matter. Today you have delivered yourself into my hands. I have the power of life or death over you, Maul. Someday, you will hold that power over another. It is the honor of the Sith. You will devote yourself to the idea of domination."

Confused, I ask him about the other apprentice. But there is no other apprentice. It had been a lie.

"You have passed the test," Lord Sidious tells me.

I deactivate my lightsaber and shove it into my belt. I taste my Master's blood on my lips. The world is returning to me slowly. My rage is ebbing, but I have not fully grasped what has happened.

My Master fixes his gaze on me, the ice-gaze that holds such power.

"From this day forward, you are a Sith Lord. You have chosen the path of darkness, the path of power. You are Lord Maul. You are my instrument."

"Yes, Master."

"Your rage," he says. "You enjoyed it? You enjoyed wanting to kill me?"

"I took great pleasure in it," I say.

He laughs again. But this time, his laughter does not mock me. "You will do well, Lord Maul," he says.

And my rage against him leaves, never to return. I am a Sith Lord. I am his instrument.

My Master takes me back to Coruscant. I am tended by a medical droid. The days pass quickly. I am determined to get better and be stronger than before. The initiation has turned me to bone and sinew. I have been emptied out and filled again with anger and purpose. I am harder than I've ever been before.

When I have recovered completely, my Master sends for me.

"You are a formidable warrior, Lord Maul," he tells me. "Now you need a weapon to match."

He shows me the Sith archives for the first time. He has perused them for long hours and found an overlooked entry. Thousand of years ago, a Sith Lord fashioned a double-ended lightsaber.

My Master points to the entry. "This will be your weapon, Lord Maul. In order to serve me well, you must be invincible."

He tells me I must build it myself so that I know it intimately. It shall be fitted to my hand, balanced for my stroke. I shall train with it until it is part of me. And then I will join him on the greatest mission of all.

"What is that, Master?" I dare to ask.

"The domination of the entire galaxy," he tells me.

That day, I feel a savage exhilaration close to the joy I feel in battle. I am involved in great things. Domination. Control.

I am only beginning to taste the dark power of a Sith.

The little rest I got during the night revives me. My wound is stiff, but my powers of recuperation are remarkable. The probe droids have not sent back any readings, but I am certain that they will this day. I can feel the disturbance in the dark side. There is a power of good on the planet, a concentration of the Force.

The Jedi are near. The anticipation I feel is like a ravenous hunger.

The twin suns of Tatooine rise. Within an hour, the heat is stifling. I hike to the nearby mesa where I can see for kilometers. A sea of coarse sand surrounds me. The two suns overhead broil the earth, sending waves of heat upward that batter against my body like solid walls. The light is blinding.

Yet Tatooine is the kind of planet I prefer. I feel

comfortable with its harshness. It operates out-side the Senate's laws. It's full of criminals and drifters, but they crowd into the spaceports. Vast areas of the planet are left to hide in. Stealth is currently my best weapon against the Jedi.

But I grow impatient waiting to hear from the probe droids. The hours crawl by. I prowl around the ship restlessly.

Sith are never restless. Our discipline is no less absolute in delay than in action.

But Master, I have never been so close before!

Finally, I settle myself into a meditation pose. I focus on the darkness within. I start with an image of a battle fought on a mission for my Master. I don't remember my opponent's face, but I remember how he fought. I remember how he tried to elude me in the end, and how I ran him down. My anger and pleasure mix and rise to a furious pitch.

Then another memory comes to my mind. I am a small boy, walking with my Master on a planet that is all ice and snow. The wind cuts like a laser as we walk by a deep blue lake, but I am warmly dressed and don't feel the cold. I have just com-pleted a series of exercises, rigorous ones that conclude with my having to run up the icy sheer slope of a mountain and come down at top speed. The effort called for superior balance and control. I feel fear, but I perform well, and I am hoping my

Master will praise me. Instead, my Master raises a hand, and suddenly the dark side picks up my small body and tosses me into the middle of the lake.

I sink and then fight my way to the surface. Chunks of ice surround me. The water is so cold I can't catch my breath. It stings my exposed skin. I remember the shock of fear I felt as I realize my thick clothes, my heavy boots, will drag me down and I will drown.

Turn your fear to anger, Maul.

That had been my lesson. I see that I have not learned it to his satisfaction.

I struggle, gulping the icy water, going down and rising again. I try to call for help. I see my Master on the shore. He does not raise a hand.

My fear becomes anger. The dark side propels my arms and legs, makes me push against the water furiously, allows me to kick my feet in my heavy boots and swim to shore. I drag myself upright, shivering.

Still he does not praise me. We merely continue our walk.

Those memories feed the dark side. I concentrate the suffering I felt and turn it to anger. Soon I find a powerful stillness in the darkness.

When my mediation is over, I exit the ship for one of my routine checks. This time, I find bantha tracks. One bantha has made a slow circle around the ship, paused, then circled again. I had not heard a sound.

I crouch to examine the tracks. The nature of the movement tells me that the bantha is carrying a passenger. Why else would an animal circle a ship?

Who is watching me?

It could be Jedi, or a spy sent by the Jedi. It could be an innocent observer. In any case, I decide to investigate. My presence here must remain secret.

I follow the bantha tracks through the soft sand. The two suns are directly overhead, and the heat is so intense it feels like flame. The wound in my leg begins to throb after a few kilometers. I ignore it.

The tracks lead me over the dunes and into a canyon. The sheer cliff walls tower over me, shielding me from the suns' rays. The walls create blue shadows. It is hard, after the brilliance of the light bouncing off the sand, to distinguish shadow from substance.

I notice that the bantha tracks go off over the rocks. I have followed them as far as I can. My eyes scan the canyon overhead. Empty. All I can see is the wide sky. The wind sweeps through the canyon, sending sand pattering against my clothes. I realize that if I were not Maul, a Sith

Lord, but an ordinary being, I would feel trapped here in this desolation. But I am a Sith. Something is wrong. I am not trapped, but am I meant to be?

Suddenly, one riderless bantha lurches into sight around a canyon wall. My concentration is broken for only a second. And in that second a Tusken Raider takes shape from a shadow under the cliff and races toward me, brandishing his gaderffii stick.

Of course I briefed myself before I left Coruscant on what I would find on Tatooine. I know about Tusken Raiders. Locals call them Sand People. They are aggressive, fierce attackers. Well adapted to the desert, they wear sand-colored robes, breath masks, and eye protectors. Their weapon of choice, the gaderffii, is double-ended like my lightsaber and glints with metal sharpened to a lethal edge. I hear that the local people fear them. They merely bore me.

I activate one end of my lightsaber, waiting for the Raider to get to me. I am almost weary at the prospect of this battle. Really, if one has to fight, it's more interesting to have a challenge.

He rushes at me, all aggression without finesse, honking an odd battle cry. With one deft stroke, I cut his gaderffii in two.

The tiresome creature roars and shakes the half that is left. He charges me again.

Instead of attacking, I follow his every move

with my lightsaber, blocking it. I can tell which way he will move before he strikes. He tips it off in so many feeble ways — by his balance, the position of his shoulders, his posture.

He roars even louder in frustration at my game. It is time to finish this.

To draw out your victory is foolish. Get the killing done. Then move on.

But as I gather myself for a combination move that will strike him down, several other Sand People suddenly appear out of nowhere. They spill out from behind dunes, underneath sand, from what appear to be mere cracks in the cliff face.

It is then that I recall another lesson about the Sand People: they travel in single file to hide their numbers.

There are at least thirty of them. They are all heading for me.

ENTRY EIGHT

Impossible as it may seem, I have made an error. Out of impatience or a residue of exhaustion, who can say.

The Sand People advance on me angrily. In their breath masks and goggles they are protected from the sand that now stings my eyes and clogs my mouth.

The howling intensifies. The Raiders shake their gaderffii and begin to surround me. There are just too many of them. I can take out four or five in the flicker of an eyelash, but that will just infuriate the rest.

Frustration boils inside me. These interruptions deflect me from my mission.

I never run away from a battle. But this one will tax me, and my strength is needed for the Jedi. If my Master hears I have been wounded, he will be furious.

All of these calculations race through my mind, faster than the Tusken Raiders are moving. One fierce Raider is the first to come at me, racing forward with his stick held high. It is easy for me to fake a dodge to the left, then make a half turn and kick him from behind as he staggers, surprised that there is now empty air where I had been standing.

He falls hard, spraying sand. This gratifies me, but it does not please his companions.

The Tusken Raiders have maneuvered me closer to the sheer face of the canyon wall. They think they have trapped me. They plan to take their time slicing me to ribbons, enjoying what they think is my fear.

At that moment, my wrist comlink sends off an alert signal. One of the probe droids has found something. The noise splits the eerie silence in the canyon. Even the Tusken Raiders pause.

The Jedi have been located. I must get back to the Infiltrator.

I turn my back to them, but only for an instant. I run straight for the canyon wall. I don't have much distance to cover, so I have to run fast. I feel the tearing wound in my left thigh, but I push it aside. Pain is another annoyance. It will not slow me down.

I run up the sheer wall, calling up the dark side to escape my enemies. My contempt and my anger at the Tusken Raiders help me. I am able to scale the wall despite the pain. With a final burst of strength that sends red agony through my leg, I flip over backward, fly over the surprised upturned faces of the Raiders, and land behind them.

They are so startled they don't react. That gives me a head start. I take off through the canyon, heading back to my ship. My wound troubles me, but now my annoyance is toward myself for feeling it. I force myself to run with my usual strength and speed.

They are no match for me. They chase me, shaking their gaderffii sticks, but they cannot catch me. I am a streak of darkness, faster than light.

I make it back to the ship. I see out the windshield that the Tusken Raiders stand a hundred meters away. They talk among themselves, waving their arms. But I know they'll give up, and they do. They trudge off, looking for easier prey.

The droid appears a few minutes later. I check its readout. One Jedi was spotted in Mos Espa. The coordinates indicate that he is heading out of the spaceport. He is most likely returning to his ship.

Jedi, I hope you are complacent right now. I hope you think you are safe for the moment. I know your arrogance tells you that you are a match for whoever is looking for you. Your surprise will add to my pleasure when I destroy you.

Technology pleases me. I personally retrofitted my speeder bike with an advanced ignition system. It is agile and fast. The Jedi don't have a chance of outrunning me.

I speed over the desert floor. The heat slams down on me, and I'm glad. It will slow the Jedi. I bend over, eyes focused on the landscape ahead, searching for the movement that will show me my enemy. All I see is sand and dirt and dunes. Yellow ground, blue sky.

The background of the battle will be almost as crucial as the battle itself. The sand will make my footing difficult. But I must turn every obstacle into an advantage. I will use the softness of the ground to weaken the Jedi, make them clumsy. I am never clumsy.

A puff of sand alerts me. I see a spot on the horizon. As I speed closer, the spot separates in two. To my surprise, it is a man and a small boy. For a moment, I am confused. Is this my prey?

Then I watch how the grown man moves, and I know the figure in the distance is indeed a Jedi. But what is he doing with that boy?

The boy . . . there is something about the boy. I sense ripples in the Force around him. Yet it is unfocused, uncontrolled. Why is he with the Jedi?

Motivations are uninteresting. Results are what matter. I have one Jedi in my sights. This Jedi will lead me to the other. Even dead, he will lead me, for the other will return to find him, and I will be waiting.

I gain on them. My engine is almost silent. I could knock the Jedi down and start from there. Or would it be more satisfying to leap from the bike and engage him directly?

I want to see his eyes.

The Jedi picks up his pace. The boy lags behind. He is in the way, so I plan to smash into him.

I am almost on them when the Jedi turns and sees me. He shouts something to the boy, and without looking or hesitating one moment, the boy falls flat on the ground. How peculiar, I note as I zoom over his prostrate form. Most boys would have hesitated or turned. His instincts are sharp for one so young. Perhaps the Force is more focused than I thought.

As soon as I am past, I dismiss the boy contemptuously. He is nothing. The Jedi is my prey.

Yes, Jedi. See where your overblown reputation will leave you. Dead at my feet.

In one perfect movement I cut the engine and leap off the speeder, my lightsaber activated and in my hand. The Jedi meets my first blow, blocking it. He has expected my flying maneuver.

If an opponent can read you, the fight is over. I don't like that the Jedi was perfectly prepared for my first blow. Within seconds, I throw away my usual combinations and strategies. This Jedi seems to know how I will move before I do.

But he cannot match my strength. I sense this. And I feel his surprise at this. Yet he does not let his puzzlement slow him down. I tell myself that this man has never met an enemy like me before, and it frightens him.

Your fear is justified. Prepare to die.

I accelerate my pace, calling on my anger to increase my power. My footwork has never been so brilliant. I use the shifting sand as resistance. My lightness and quickness will defeat this man, with his large body, his heavy movements.

But he is graceful, this Jedi. The sand doesn't seem to hamper him. He is never off balance, no matter where or how I strike.

Our blows send shudders through my body. He meets my strength. Our lightsabers clash and sizzle. Dust and sand rise around us. I never lose my rhythm.

The Jedi calls to the boy, tells him to go back to the ship. The cowardly boy runs off. After I defeat my enemy, I will find the second Jedi.

But I must confess that this Jedi is a challenge. If I leap, he is with me. If I turn, he follows me. He meets my ferocity with his own. His lightsaber swirls and hums, and several times comes closer than I like.

It is because of my wound. It has slowed me down somewhat. It is almost imperceptible, but it is there. The Jedi has an advantage. I am not at my best.

This realization sends more rage pumping into my body. I am angry at myself, but I use the anger to fuel the dark side. I feel the Force come from the Jedi and I send it back to him, showing him that I, too, have a connection, and it is stronger than his. I launch a furious counterattack. I feel the Jedi beginning to tire, and triumph rises like a red mist before my eyes. I gain the advantage. I am winning. I will defeat him.

I have been surprised at his skill, but now I am confident of victory. I will savor each moment of this battle.

Even through his fatigue, his blows still have power. He is a large man with impressive strength. He will fall heavily, like a monument.

I feel a savage pleasure course through me. His weakness feeds my power. I drive him back, spin around when he parries, drive him back again. The dust chokes my throat, but I don't notice it.

Suddenly, the ship is here. And in the blink of an eye, I lose sight of the Jedi. Does he disappear in the dust? Flip past me? I am still not sure.

Had I maneuvered him where I wanted him?

Or had he maneuvered me?

I see him make a gigantic leap and land on the ramp of the ship.

No! I am after him, but I am too late.

I stand and watch the ship as it rises. Soon it is just a speck in the distance.

I taste sand in my mouth. The Jedi is gone.

I stand in the same spot for a long time. The wind rises. It drives the sand against me furiously, sharp pricks against my face and exposed skin. I feel something trickle into my mouth: blood. Still I stand and let the wind whip the sand in a maelstrom around me and against me.

The blood in my mouth stings, tasting of humiliation. Shame. I have not felt shame like this before. It is a darkness darker than any I have known. But it is not a pleasing darkness.

I have failed. Now I must tell my Master.

There is no reason to remain on Tatooine. I know what I must do. I must return to Coruscant and face Lord Sidious. I send a report that the Jedi have taken off with the Queen, and I am returning. I know my Master will want to hear the details in person.

I am prepared to do this, but I do not look forward to it. I have brought him bad news once before. My successes have been spectacular, but on one mission, I had to report failure.

It was in the early days when Lord Sidious was secretly working to consolidate the strength of the Trade Federation. My mission was to go to the planet Chryya and ensure that their thriving spice business would be turned over to the Trade Federation to manage. I would accomplish this through threats and intimidation. I would not reveal my Sith powers unless I left my opponent dead.

At first, I was successful. A few incidents convinced the frightened merchants to sign all the agreements. But then one merchant organized a protest. Before I could move against him, a groundswell grew among the people. Every citizen of Chryya destroyed their spice supplies rather than give in to the Trade Federation. They wrecked their economy for principle.

I had not forseen this. In my experience, creatures are guided by their own comforts. I could not kill the entire population, so I had to leave and report my failure to my Master.

He did not take it well. He raised a hand, and the dark side grabbed me by the throat and lifted me high. My breath was squeezed out of me slowly. Too slowly. I had time to feel every stretched-out moment of panic as I struggled to force even the tiniest trickle of air into my lungs.

When I was close to passing out, I was dropped to the floor in a heap. My Master walked away. He did not address me or call for me for some time. The removal of his favor was worse than the punishment.

So on the journey back, I consider how much of my story to tell. I question whether it is necessary to tell him of my battle with the pirates, or my encounter with the Sand People. If I do, I will have to confess that I sustained a leg wound. I do not want to show weakness in front of my Master.

And my leg is almost healed. There is no reason to tell him.

He will blame me for allowing myself to get caught in the pirate's snare. He won't listen if I try to tell him it was impossible to avoid them. He will cut me off.

I don't want excuses. Only results.

Sometimes explanations are not excuses, yet they sound that way. And sometimes stories are better left untold.

I do not like concealing something from my Master. I've never done it before. But I tell myself that any questioning of me would only distract him. We must focus on the next step.

I arrive at Coruscant at night. When I come out of hyperspace, the light of the planet dazzles my eyes like an impossibly bright star. At night it glows from the millions of lights that bounce off the atmosphere. Some say it is the most beautiful sight in the galaxy.

I do not know, or care, about beauty. Apprehension fizzes in my blood. There is nothing in the galaxy to compare to my Master when he is displeased.

I dock my ship in the landing bay. The entrance panel slides closed. To outsiders it looks like a sheer wall. I complete my arrival checks. When I realize that I am delaying, I wrench my mind into the proper form for a Sith Lord. We do not delay. We do not feel dread.

I head straight for my Master. He sits in the middle of an empty room, the place where he plans and meditates. There is nothing in the room to distract him. Even the door slides closed and becomes invisible.

I relate what happened. How I raced to find the Jedi, how I was close to defeating him, how he leaped onto the ramp of the ship.

My Master is wearing his hood, so I cannot see his eyes. I rely on his mouth and skin tone to tell me if he's angry, but I see no change.

"You feel you would have defeated this Jedi?" he asks.

"Yes, Master. I felt him tire. I can defeat him."

"Was he bearded?"

I nod.

"Good. That is Qui-Gon Jinn. He is the stronger of the two."

My Master seems satisfied. This puzzles me. Surely he is furious at me for allowing the Jedi to escape.

I venture my guess that the Jedi and the Queen will come to Coruscant. What else can she do? She is young and looks to authority. She will be naïve enough to think that the Senate can help her. I am pleased with my deduction, but it does not seem to interest my Master.

He waves his hand and tells me that she is already here.

She is close by, staying in the Senatorial quarters.

I stiffen. "And the Jedi?"

They are on Coruscant as well.

My hand goes to the hilt of my lightsaber. My enemy is near. A burning begins in my chest and spreads outward.

"Let me kill them, Master."

"Not here," he says. He seems preoccupied, as though I am not even in the room. "I have another plan."

While in my Master's presence, I was relieved at my lack of punishment. Obviously, his mind is on other things.

But as soon as I am alone, I wonder. Is my Master reviving an old method used when I was young, delaying punishment until my nerves are screaming? I never knew when my punishment would come, or what it would be. Then when it came, I would almost feel relief.

But never for long. As soon as the punishment began, relief was but a memory. I am too old now to be frightened by a roomful of dinkos, but I never underestimate my Master's ingenuity.

Did he know of my battle with the pirates, my foolish decision to follow those bantha tracks? Did he sense my leg wound? Both of these episodes put me in danger and slowed me down. Is he waiting until I am complacent to fling my mistakes in my face?

Think of the now, Maul. Think of the future. Do not meditate on the past.

I must use my shame. I must turn it inward to make the darkness in me grow. My shame will feed my hatred. That will make me stronger, and when I meet my enemy again, I will be ready.

And now my enemy has a name. Qui-Gon Jinn.

In the past I never cared about the name of my enemy. My enemy was a target, nothing more. Knowing his name for any other purpose than tracking was valueless.

But I am glad now to be able to name my enemy. *Qui-Gon Jinn.* I repeat the name to myself with hatred in every syllable, chant it like a curse.

I will destroy you, Qui-Gon Jinn. I will see the shock in your eyes when I run you through, Qui-Gon Jinn. I will stand over your dead body in triumph, Qui-Gon Jinn.

Because of you, I have failed my Master.

You will pay.

My Master calls me to him and tells me that Queen Amidala has attempted to bring the Senate to her cause, just as we expected. She has asked them to outlaw the Trade Federation blockade of Naboo. She has failed, just as we expected.

He chortles with triumph, in the best mood I've ever seen him. It is a satisfying thing, he says, when every piece of your plan falls into place, thanks to your guile and the stupid, unknowing cooperation of your pawns.

I feel relief. My Master doesn't know about my leg wound, about the Togorian pirates. He is vibrating with triumph, ready to take the next step. My mistakes don't matter. Unless he is distracted by good news and will turn on me later . . .

"She is going back to Naboo," he says harshly. "Foolish girl. The Jedi accompany her." He smiles. "Come. Let us contact the Neimoidians and share the good news."

He dons his robe and hood and activates the holocomm. Nute Gunray responds almost immediately. His eyes are fearful as he glimpses Darth Sidious. I stay out of sight.

My Master tells Nute that the Queen is on her way back to Naboo. Nute is surprised, but he does not fear her arrival.

"When she gets there, destroy her," my Master says.

Nute nods. This is not hard for him to accomplish. He has troops and guards and assassin droids. He won't have to dirty his hands.

Lord Sidious asks if the planet is secure. Nute rushes to assure him that it is. The Trade Federation has taken over the last pocket of primitives. They are in complete control.

I wait, hoping, knowing what my Master will say. It is my time. He needs me now. I must redeem myself. He must give me the chance to bring down Qui-Gon Jinn.

"I am sending Darth Maul to join you. He will deal with the Jedi."

I see Nute swallow. He darts a quick look at Rune. They are not pleased at the thought of my company.

But they nod and pretend that they are.

The screen goes black. My Master laughs.

"Soon the Neimoidians will no longer be useful to us," he says. "What a happy day that will be."

He turns. His eyes command me. "Make sure the Neimoidians take care of Queen Amidala. You yourself must destroy the Jedi. Do not fail me again."

Terror rises off Nute Gunray and Rune Haako like steam. I intimidate them without saying a word. It is clear the minute I arrive on Naboo. Is it my ritual tattoos, my silence, my eyes? All I have to do is look in their direction and they scurry away.

So I look in their direction often.

I find on my arrival that Nute and Rune have settled into the Theed palace as though it had been built just for them. Nute has taken over Queen Amidala's private bedroom. They think that they will be rewarded for their loyalty with the control of Naboo.

It is true that the Neimoidians are still useful to us. But it's also important for our lackeys to know who is really in charge.

So on the morning I arrive, I stride into the Queen's bedroom, where Nute snoozes on her sleep-couch, covered by a blanket woven of soft shimmersilk. I yank off the coverlet and kick him. Hard.

He wakes in a panic. "Are they invading?"

What a fool he is. Disgusted, I tell him to clear out.

"These are now my quarters," I say.

His eyes dart in fear. He tries at the last moment to take the shimmersilk cover, but I grab it from his hands. It tears in half, and I note the dismay on Nute's face. I rend it further just to scare him. Then I fling the pieces in his face.

"Send someone to remove the traces of your presence here," I snap.

He runs as fast as a Neimoidian is capable, anxious to get out of my sight.

As soon as he is gone, I laugh. It's not that I want to sleep in luxury. But I do enjoy terrifying Nute. It's too easy, but it's pleasurable.

I walk through the palace, noting the richness of the materials, the fine workmanship of the furnishings, the grandeur of the hallways and staircases. Windows run floor to ceiling and reflect back the pools and waterfalls of the city of Theed. I do not often notice my surroundings except as something to move through and exploit in order to accomplish a mission. But here I begin to see what lies ahead for us. Control of the galaxy in our grasp, with every luxury at our feet.

I have been raised without luxury. Bare walls,

bare floors, a sleep-mat. A bowl to eat from. I have believed fine things make one soft. All my joy comes in battle, all my pleasure comes in preparing for it.

But I could be wrong about this. I could rule from a palace like this one day. It would not be so terrible a fate.

I find the throne room. Nute and Rune are talking, and they stop abruptly when I appear in the doorway. No doubt Nute was complaining about me.

I stroll in and look at Nute hard. He rises off the throne and hurries to a low chair. I sit, and they glance at me nervously.

"Status report," I tell them.

Nute blathers that things are going well on Naboo. Rune chimes in that the people are cowed completely in the camps. The underground resistance movement is small and will be crushed any day. Every ship in the area, every troop has been alerted to watch out for the Queen's ship. She will be spotted as soon as she enters Naboo's atmosphere, they promise. She will no doubt land in the central square, hoping to negotiate, with the Jedi as her shields. It is impossible for her to slip through the many safeguards they have set up.

"Unless she is already here," I say.

"Impossible!" They cry this in one voice.

I suggest that together we check out security around the plaza. This meets with their usual glassy-eyed, babbling approval.

We stroll around the central plaza. Waterfalls thunder nearby. Their spray cools the air. The plaza is wide and desolate. I imagine that before the invasion it would have been full of people. I have heard of the fine crafts of Naboo, the musicians, the food sellers, all the pleasures that could be bought or traded for in the center of the great city.

I prefer it empty.

Nute and Rune point out the patrols. They are timed to cover the plaza every fifteen minutes.

"Make it every five," I say.

Rune points out nervously that there are still pockets of resistance throughout the city. Shouldn't we keep the troops spread out?

I let my gaze squeeze their puny minds, turn their thoughts liquid with fear.

"Do you think," I ask in a dangerous tone, "the Queen will dawdle when she arrives, and simply wait for you to pick her up? Think, cretin. Where do you think she'll be heading?"

Nute barks the order into his comlink. Five-minute patrols! He has begun to fidget.

"There should be surveillance at all times," I say, sweeping my arm to take in the balconies. "Infrared sensors to alert the patrols."

Rune tells me quickly that they will arrange it.

The Queen cannot escape their surveillance. Everything is under control —

Nute's comlink signals. He hesitates.

I suggest he answer it, or he'll find himself thrown over a waterfall.

An officer reports in from the field. The Queen's ship has been found in the Naboo swamps.

Nute looks stunned. Rune's ugly mouth drops open. Their stupidity is no longer amusing.

"Have you captured her?" Nute roars.

The officer replies that the ship is empty, and there is no sign of the Queen's party. They have disappeared.

I say nothing. It is more effective.

Nute's voice trembles as he orders the officer to send out patrols to search.

I grab his comlink and switch it off. There is no reason to hear more dithering from fools. I hold it in front of his face.

"Everything is under control, you say?" I hiss directly in his face. He flinches. "You'll pay for this. Now we must contact Lord Sidious."

Nute nods. He has no choice. But the mere mention of my Master's name has made him look greener than usual. Things are slipping out of his control. When my Master first contacted the Neimoidians to suggest the blockade, their greed overcame them. They thought this would be easy, no doubt. Now I sense that Nute and Rune wish they were on a planet in the Outer Rim, well away from the Sith Lord's grasp. Only their fear and greed keep them tethered here.

Lord Sidious appears before us in hologram form. Nute repeats the officer's report, adding that he has acted quickly to send out search patrols.

"This is an unexpected move for her," Lord Sidious says. "It is too aggressive . . . Lord Maul, be mindful."

He tells me to let them make the first move. Whatever it may be, whenever it may come, I will be ready.

Yes, Qui-Gon Jinn. I will wait for you to make your move. That will leave you open. We will meet each other soon.

For me, patience has never been easy. To calm my mind, I concentrate on the battle I know is ahead. When I reach out to gather the dark side of the Force around me, it is unsettled, turbulent. I know my enemy is near.

My first blow will entice you, Qui-Gon Jinn. My second blow will be the true blow, the one that will stagger you. I know your fighting style now. I know how quickly you can move, and how strong your stroke is. I know that your instincts are good, and that you are fast. None of this will save you. I will push you until you weaken, just as I did before. And when your guard slips for just a fraction of a moment, I'll strike the death blow.

My hatred is as cold and hard as the stone of the palace floor. It lies inside my chest. I animate it, feed it so that it grows.

A voice pounds in my head, the voice of my Master. It reminds me not to fail.

I remember the gray-blue eyes of the Jedi. There was fierceness there, but distance, too. He saw me, but he also saw through me. He fought me, but he did not hate me.

I will make him hate me.

Nute runs toward me. I am annoyed at the interruption. I turn to him angrily.

"She is assembling an army!" he cries.

At least the Neimoidian patrols do some good. They discover that Queen Amidala has contacted the primitives in the swamp.

I point out to Nute that he told us the primitives had all been rounded up.

"They went into hiding!" he exclaims. "They know the terrain better than we do. . . ."

I silence him with a look. Explanations are excuses. I see that now.

The Gungans are assembling an army. Nute and Rune aren't worried so much about this. The primitives are no match for the Trade Federation forces. The droid army and its weaponry are invincible.

What Queen Amidala is planning is less clear. Is she planning to fight? Will she ride at the head of the Gungan army? That thought makes me laugh. She will last ten seconds in such a battle. Naboo has no forces to speak of. All of her starfighters have been captured. Her volunteer pilots and officers are in camps. What does she think she can accomplish, depending on primitives with their tiny brains?

And what of the Jedi? Will they ride beside her? Do they really think they can protect her against thousands of battle droids?

I contact my Master. This is news he must hear.

Lord Sidious doesn't flinch as I report the news. He is somewhat surprised at the Queen's foolishness.

But now I wonder if she is being manipulated by the Jedi. Perhaps they have some plan in mind. I don't think the young Queen is wise enough to plot her own strategy. They must be involved.

Lord Sidious rejects my speculation. The Jedi are forbidden to engage in a conflict. They are advisors and protectors, nothing more. And Qui-Gon Jinn would not violate his covenant.

"This will work to our advantage," he says.

My Master sees farther than I can. The pieces fall into place for him. Of course he is right. The Jedi always abide by their rules. That will be their downfall. They cannot win against the Sith, who have no rules but domination.

"Wipe them out," Lord Sidious tells us. "All of them."

We will.

I feel the movement of the dark side as a wave that begins as a ripple and gathers momentum until it towers and crashes against my body, sucking the oxygen from my lungs.

Qui-Gon Jinn is here. He is in Theed.

At last I shall meet my enemy.

Should I kill him first, or kill his apprentice before his eyes? Will I grind his face in sorrow before I finish him?

I will let the battle dictate. I will not plan too much.

I rise smoothly. I activate both ends of my lightsaber, double-checking my equipment, making a few passes to test it. Then I return the lightsaber to my belt.

I close my eyes and focus on the image of my enemy. I have time. Either sensors or the Trade Federation troops will locate the Jedi.

All my life I have waited. All my life I have trained. And here is the moment. My experiences, my knowledge, my instincts — they have all converged on this day, on this world, for my ultimate test.

Even my failure to kill the Jedi on Tatooine only serves as a step toward his defeat. I will use everything I have.

Since I was a boy, I have done everything my Master asked. I have fulfilled task after task, com-pleted mission after mission. Yet I know nothing else matters in the face of this. Today is the day I shall truly prove myself.

I will tear Qui-Gon Jinn apart. My Master will see that I am indeed invincible. He will have no need to punish me, to doubt me, ever again.

Because I do not doubt myself. I know I will not fail. Sith do not fail. It is not overconfidence I feel, but certainty.

The sensors have reported back. They have been spotted in the spaceport central hangar. Nute and Rune have barricaded themselves in the palace. They are cowards, but even I imagine they can hold the palace against the puny assault of the Queen.

I am ready. Know this: I will seal Qui-Gon Jinn's fate, and the fate of his apprentice, Obi-Wan Kenobi. I will stand over their dead bodies. I will spill their blood. Their defeat will taste like honey in my mouth. And then I will bring their lightsabers back to my Master and lay them at his feet. He will see what I can do.

And then we shall rule the galaxy together, side by side. We are Sith Lords. No one can defeat us.

EPILOGUE

VOICE RECORDING

BY: LORD DARTH SIDIOUS

LOCATION: CORUSCANT

I regret to announce that Lord Maul was wrong. A Sith Lord can be defeated if he is an apprentice who falls victim to his belief in his own invincibility.

I take up the task of completing the journal of my deceased apprentice, Lord Darth Maul. Here I shall record what I learned of his death at the hands of the Jedi, Obi-Wan Kenobi.

Lord Maul's information was correct: the Queen and a small force had invaded the central hangar. Their object was to steal back Naboo starfighters in order to knock out the orbiting Droid Control Ship. This should have been clear to Maul. He should have prevented the ships from taking off. Instead, he focused on the Jedi. These were his orders, but he should have realized a shift in plan was called for.

My apprentice was worthy, but he was never

flexible. He focused on the Jedi for personal revenge. I had drilled single-mindedness into my apprentice from an early age. I did not expect it would become a failing.

Several of the ships escaped the hangar. Queen Amidala left for the palace to complete the next step of the plan that I must now ruefully admit was rather bold. It depended too much on luck, but the outcome proves the plan, doesn't it?

The Jedi remained to fight Lord Maul. No doubt they knew that he was the only one capable of stopping the Queen.

Here was Lord Maul's mistake: if he could not dispatch them quickly, he should have gone to the palace to deal with the Queen. I do not like the fact that she is still alive. . . .

As for my disappointing apprentice, he met the Jedi in combat. From the report I received he fought well — brilliantly, in fact. It amuses me to think of the Jedi's surprise at the deadly skill of the Sith. Now they know that we have returned, and they must suspect they are no match for us. Fear must curdle inside them now. Fear is an unfamiliar feeling to a Jedi.

Now they must live with it.

The battle began in the hangar. Darth Maul activated his double-ended lightsaber, a weapon he fashioned himself under my supervision. In his hands this weapon was flawless — or so I thought.

He made the Jedi run. They had to use everything they knew and more to meet his skill. They went at him, two on one, and they could not defeat him. No doubt Maul used his formidable dark powers to blunt their use of the Force.

The battle raged out of the hangar and into the Theed main power generator. It is built with catwalks that run around many levels. Now they were alone, fighting what they all knew would be a death fight.

You wonder how I know what transpired here. It is my job to know everything that affects my plan to take over the galaxy. There are ways to find out anything. Even what lies in the hearts and minds of living beings. My knowledge gives me power. And I do not need to reveal how I come by it.

Qui-Gon Jinn took the lead. A powerful warrior, I suspect he surprised Maul with his stamina. At one point Qui-Gon scored a hit and Maul fell several levels. But by the time the Jedi jumped down to engage him again, my apprentice had gained his feet and fought back with not one bit of energy displaced.

Lord Maul should have told me about his battle with the Togorian pirates. I have read his journal, and I see that he kept a secret from me. If I had known about his leg wound, would I have given different orders, arranged for a backup?

No. I am sure Maul was at his peak when he

fought the Jedi. His error was of miscalculation, not weakness. A mental failing, not a physical one. Whether I could have foreseen that is a question I cannot answer.

There aren't many of those.

At last the battle reached a hallway of deadly laser walls. The force fields separated the Jedi from Maul, and from each other. They had to wait until the walls retracted before engaging in the next stage of the battle.

I do not know if it was luck or skill that set the stage for the final confrontation. Did Maul succeed in separating the Jedi, or did he take advantage of a situation he found himself in? Either way, he performed well.

Now he was one-on-one with Qui-Gon Jinn. A frustrated Obi-Wan was trapped behind the energy walls. It must have been a source of satisfaction for Maul to meet Qui-Gon again. I know he felt shame at his failure on Tatooine. Here was vindication and pleasure for him, a sweet triumph. My apprentice always did receive a peculiar joy from battle.

The duel escalated to a ferocity that taxed the powers of the Jedi. Maul, I am sure, was under control at all times.

Do not neglect old tricks, apprentice. They work.

The battle with Qui-Gon ended with a simple

move, a trick: Using the hilt of a lightsaber to knock an opponent under the chin. Maul usually disdained such blunt maneuvers. He is — was — an elegant fighter. Precise. But when he saw his opening, no doubt he remembered my lesson.

A blow to Qui-Gon's chin left him dazed.

Push your advantage always.

Maul's lightsaber whirled, and ran Qui-Gon Jinn through. The Jedi Master fell.

I can imagine young Obi-Wan's scream. If I chuckle, it is only because the arrogance of the Jedi order infuriates me. How I love to deflate them. How much delicious pleasure I get from picturing that moment, when the apprentice saw the Master fall.

This was my victory as much as Lord Maul's, for it was thanks to my teaching, my training, that he was able to defeat the great Qui-Gon Jinn.

The defeat of such an opponent should have cooled his mind, sharpened his focus. But instead, Maul met his undoing: the young Obi-Wan Kenobi. I am sure Maul knew the apprentice would attack with great savagery on behalf of his Master. He would have been prepared for that.

But I fear that Maul underestimated Obi-Wan's control. At first, Maul was winning. The defeat of Obi-Wan was in his grasp. Maul knocked him into the melting pit. Obi-Wan hung by a small nozzle that protruded from the sheer wall. It would have been an easy job to dislodge his grip, knock him thousands of meters down into the pit, and end the life of another nuisance of a Jedi.

Instead, Maul gloated. He contemptuously kicked Obi-Wan's lightsaber into the pit. He paced in front of the stricken Jedi, snarling. No doubt my apprentice wanted to savor the moment. Against all my teaching, he hesitated in order to revel in his triumph.

The battle is not over until your opponent is dead.

How often had I drilled that into him?

Obi-Wan called on the Force. He leaped from the pit, Qui-Gon's lightsaber flying to his hand. Maul did not have enough time to parry the blow that must have been the last, great surprise of his life.

My worthy apprentice failed me in the end. He fell into the melting pit. I am glad, at least, that his body was consumed. If there must be an end, it is a fitting one.

Time and again I told him not to underestimate the Jedi. At the end, he did. Now he is dispersed to the far ends of the galaxy.

Meanwhile, the Queen had invaded the palace. She tricked Rune and Nute by using a decoy. Just remembering this makes me feel weary. I could always count on Neimoidian stupidity, but usually it worked to my advantage.

Another battle raged overhead, high in the atmosphere of Naboo. Starfighters tried to hit the main control ship piloted by the Neimoidians. One of the starfighters was piloted by the slave boy Qui-Gon Jinn had spirited off Tatooine for some foolish compassionate reason. This boy managed to penetrate the control ship. He blew the reactor. I do not believe this was dumb luck. I will watch this boy. Maul, too, felt the Force in him. The question is whether it is too late for him to control it.

The battle droids collapsed back on Naboo. The destroyer droids deactivated at the palace. The Queen held Nute Gunray. The government was back in her hands.

Defeated by a young boy, a naïve girl, and a Jedi apprentice. It was not a good day.

But it is merely a setback, already in the past. Now the Jedi know that the Sith are still operating. No doubt they will strategize, plan to move against me. No matter. I will defeat them. I feel contempt for all of them: Yoda, Mace Windu, the young Obi-Wan. But I will not make the mistake of my apprentice. I will never forget that they can get lucky.

I do not know what to do with this account. Perhaps I will enter it into the Sith archives. Perhaps I will destroy it. It is a record of miscalculation more than anything. Lord Maul thought he was leaving a record of his cleverness and bravery. Instead, it is a record of his vanity and weakness.

Maul made mistakes of impatience and temper. In the end, he had been too hungry for victory. He had failed to expect the resilience of Obi-Wan Kenobi. He allowed his feeling of triumph to distract him.

I, too, made a mistake. Perhaps Maul was not the best choice. For my next apprentice, I will choose more carefully. There must be hate and fear in him. There must be something in his heart that has gone cold, something that I can work on to expand into ruthlessness. But there must be great cunning and intelligence as well.

The next apprentice will make no mistakes.

The time has come for a final face-off between Qui-Gon Jinn
and his first, dark apprentice, Xanatos. Qui-Gon's life — and
the life of his thirteen-year-old apprentice Obi-Wan Kenobi —
are held in the balance.

Discover How It All Began

JEDI APPRENTICE

The Captive Temple

Xanatos was perfectly still, waist-high in deep water, suspended by the Force without kicking or moving his arms. His wet black hair flowed to his shoulders and his sharp blue eyes, as clear and cold as ice crystals, gleamed in the dim light. Watery shadows sent flickering patterns across his black tunic.

Qui-Gon and Obi-Wan had already activated their lightsabers. They stood waiting.

But Xanatos didn't move to engage them. He smiled.

"It took you longer than even I imagined for you to figure out it was me," he called mockingly to Qui-Gon. "That noble head of yours can be so thick. Foolishly, I continue to give you credit for some intelligence."

Qui-Gon stood easily, his lightsaber activated but held loosely at his side. He did not appear to be in attack position, but Obi-Wan knew his fighting style well. If Xanatos were to spring, Qui-Gon had only to shift slightly in order to meet the attack.

Qui-Gon didn't answer Xanatos. His face was a study in composure. He didn't appear to have heard Xanatos at all.

Obi-Wan knew they could not attack while Xanatos remained in the water. If they jumped in after him, their lightsabers would short out if the activated lasers came into contact with the water. Xanatos knew it, too. Perhaps that was why he taunted Qui-Gon, goading him to attack.

"You don't even answer me?" he called. "Still holding a grudge? What a hard heart you have, Qui-Gon."

"I wasn't aware we were having a conversation," Qui-Gon answered. He moved forward a step. "That was always the way with you, Xanatos — you prefer the sound of your own voice."

Obi-Wan saw a momentary flush on Xanatos's cheeks. Then he laughed. "How tiresome you are, Qui-Gon. Your petty taunts still miss their mark. You never were very clever. And you still rely on children to do your work. You never would have figured out the water tunnels on your own."

Suddenly, he flew through the air in a great leap, propelled by the Force. His black cape streamed water as he activated his lightsaber in the blink of an eye. Obi-Wan was ready, stepping forward even as Xanatos touched down on the platform.

He saw Bant make a running dive off the platform. She was unarmed, and no doubt was swimming for help. She had only waited for Xanatos to move.

Xanatos's red lightsaber crashed against the green glow of Qui-Gon's. The angry buzz echoed through the tunnel. Xanatos had landed to Qui-Gon's left, and Obi-Wan raced to cover the Jedi's flank.

Xanatos was a skilled fighter. His strength was staggering. When Obi-Wan's lightsaber tangled with his, the shock nearly sent him flying backward. It was all he could do to keep his feet. The platform soon grew slick with their wet footprints and the water from their clothes. It was hard for Obi-Wan to keep his footing.

Xanatos was as quick as he was strong, already whirling away from Obi-Wan's attacks to stricke at Qui-Gon.

Gradually, Obi-Wan became aware that Qui-

Gon had succeeded in manipulating Xanatos, getting him close to the narrow stairs. Xanatos took a step down, then another, as Qui-Gon stepped up the fierceness of his attack. Obi-Wan saw the reason for the strategy. If Xanatos got close enough to the tank, he would have to swing back to gain momentum for his blows. Xanatos would run the risk of shorting out his lightsaber or weakening his attacks.

The strategy could not be obvious, he knew. They had to distract Xanatos with counter-moves so that he wouldn't realize how close he was to the water below.

Obi-Wan joined in the attempt, trying to keep Xanatos off-balance while driving him toward the water. The steps were slippery. It was difficult to get enough grounding to lend strength to his blows. He was tiring, but Qui-Gon remained focused, moving gracefully, forcing Xanatos down another step.

As he fought side by side with Qui-Gon, Obi-Wan felt the familiar rhythm pulse between them. The Force was strong, bonding them together as one unit.

Over the sound of the battle, the sizzle of the lightsabers, and his own heavy breathing, Obi-Wan heard a noise. It started as a rumble in the distance. Within seconds, it was a roar.

It was the water flushing the system. A giant

tidal wave of foaming water rushed toward them from a conduit in the tank.

"Jump, Obi-Wan," Qui-Gon ordered. Using the Force, they made a simultaneous leap onto the platform above.

Immediately, Obi-Wan whirled to face Xanatos, who was no doubt behind them.

But Xanatos had not leaped to safety. Grinning, he deactivated his lightsaber, then jumped off the step just as the torrent roared through. Within the flicker of an eyelash, he was swept away.

"He'll drown," Obi-Wan said, astonished at Xanatos's action.

"No, he won't," Qui-Gon said grimly, his eyes on the white water. "We shall meet him again."